Fisher-Price

Little People

Who's New at School?

written by Lori C. Froeb

illustrated by Pixel Mouse House

Reader's
Digest
Children's Books

New York, New York • Montréal, Québec • Bath, United Kingdom

It was almost time for school. Eddie and Sarah Lynn were having their breakfast while their mom made them lunches.
"Kids, today is our new neighbor's first day joining your class at school. Try to make him feel welcome, okay?" said their mom.

"Sure!" Eddie said. "We can introduce him to all our friends!"

A new boy had moved next door only yesterday and the twins were anxious to get to know him.

After breakfast, they all headed for the bus stop.

The boy and his father were already waiting at the corner.

"Hello!" Sarah said. "I'm Sarah Lynn and this is my brother Eddie. What's your name?"

"*Me llamo Roberto,*" the boy answered. "My name is Roberto."

"Wow! You speak another language!" said Eddie. "That's neat!"

"It is Spanish," said Roberto. "My family is from South America."

"Have a good day at school," said Roberto's dad when the bus pulled up.

"*¡Adios, papá!*" answered Roberto. "See you later!"

"Good-bye, mom!" said Eddie and Sarah Lynn together.

On the bus, Eddie and Sarah Lynn couldn't wait to introduce Roberto to all their friends. And Maggie, Michael, and Sonya Lee couldn't wait to tell him all about their teacher and classroom!

"We have class pets!" squealed Sonya Lee. "They are hamsters!"

"I love art class," added Michael. "Roberto, what is your favorite part of school?"

"I like to listen to stories," said Roberto. "My *papi* reads to me all the time."

Before class started, the teacher introduced Roberto.
"Everyone, please welcome Roberto," she said.
"Hi, Roberto!" the class cheered.
"*¡Hola a todos!*" said Roberto. "That means, 'Hello, everybody!'"

"Class, Roberto is bilingual," their teacher added. "That means he speaks two languages—English and Spanish."

Eddie raised his hand. "Roberto can sit next to me," he said.

"That's a great idea," said their teacher. "Let's start Show and Tell!"

Sonya Lee held up a brightly colored picture of mountains and a village. "This is a drawing that my pen pal Rosa sent me. She lives in Peru." There was some writing on the bottom of the picture. "What does the sentence say?" asked Michael.

Me alegro de que seamos amigos

"I don't know," said Sonya Lee. "I wish I could read it!"

"That is Spanish!" said Roberto. "It says, *'Me alegro de que seamos amigos'* or 'I'm glad we are friends!'"

"Wow," giggled Sonya Lee. "Thanks, Roberto. Now I can tell her I am glad, too!"

Everyone did their best to make Roberto feel welcome. Michael let him feed Wiggles and Nibbles even though it was his turn.

Maggie let Roberto choose the book for story time even though she already had her favorite book picked.

And Sarah Lynn let him borrow her special pencil during writing practice.

Before long it was time for lunch. "Roberto, come sit at our table!" Eddie said.

Everyone opened their lunch boxes. Sonya had a sandwich. Michael had soup. Eddie had spaghetti. Roberto had something no one had seen before.

"What are you eating?" asked Maggie.

"It's called a burrito," answered Roberto. "It is filled with beans, rice, cheese, and a sauce called salsa. It is *delicioso*–delicious!"

After lunch, it was time for recess and the class went outside to play.
Sarah Lynn and Sonya Lee were twirling a jump rope for Maggie.
"One, two, three, four," they counted as Maggie jumped.
"*Cinco, seis, siete, ocho,*" Roberto continued until Maggie stopped.

"You were counting in Spanish!" said Eddie excitedly.

"*¡Sí!* Yes! Seven, eight, nine, ten," giggled Roberto. "Let's swing on the swings—*¡el columpio!*"

"I'll race you!" shouted Michael.

When everyone was back in the classroom, the teacher handed out markers and paper. "Today, I want everyone to draw his favorite animal," the teacher explained.

Roberto drew a rabbit. "*El conejo* is the Spanish word for rabbit."

Sonya Lee drew a cat. Maggie drew a seahorse. Sarah Lynn drew a parrot. Eddie drew Freddie. Then the class heard a sound. *Ribbit! Ribbit!*

"Is that who I think it is?" Eddie said, surprised. Out popped Freddie from Eddie's backpack and the kids all laughed.

"It looks like Roberto wasn't the only new student in class today," the teacher giggled. "Welcome, Freddie!"

"Welcome, Freddie," the class cheered.

"How do you say frog in Spanish, Roberto?" asked Eddie.

"*La rana,*" answered Roberto.

"*La rana,*" repeated Eddie. "Maybe that can be Freddie's new nickname!"

Walking to the bus, the friends talked about what a great day they had.

"What do you think of our school?" asked Sarah Lynn.

"It's great! *¡Excelente!*" answered Roberto. "Thank you for helping me feel welcome."

"Good-bye, Roberto!" Eddie and Sarah Lynn said when the bus dropped them off.

"*¡Adios!*" answered Roberto. "See you tomorrow!"

Seek and Find Fun!

Can you find all these things inside the book? Look carefully!

crayon

rose

hair bow

dinosaur

bell

grapes

Let's Learn Spanish!

Roberto taught Eddie and his friends some Spanish words.
Do you remember them?

el columpio • swings

el conejo • rabbit

papi • daddy

la rana • frog